Judy Sierra

THERE'S A ZOO IN ROOM 22

Illustrated by

BARNEY SALTZBERG

GULLIVER BOOKS
HARCOURT, INC.
San Diego   New York   London

www.harcourt.com

Gulliver Books is a registered trademark of Harcourt, Inc.

Library of Congress Cataloging-in-Publication Data
Sierra, Judy.
There's a zoo in room 22/by Judy Sierra; illustrated by
Barney Saltzberg.
p. cm.
"Gulliver Books."
Summary: Each of twenty-six poems describes the antics and habits of
a zany classroom pet whose name begins with a different letter of
the alphabet.
1. Animals—Juvenile poetry.   2. Classrooms—Juvenile poetry.
3. Children's poetry, American.   4. Alphabet rhymes.   [1. Alphabet—
Poetry.   2. Schools—Poetry.   3. Animals—Poetry.
4. American poetry.]   I. Saltzberg, Barney, ill.   II. Title.
PS3569.I39T48   2000
811'.54—dc21   99-6708
ISBN 0-15-202033-0

First edition
A C E G H F D B
Printed in Hong Kong

The illustrations in this book were done in pencil, Dr. Martin's
Watercolors, and Prisma colored pencil on paper.
The display type was set in Fontesque.
The text type was set in Century 751.
Printed by South China Printing Company, Ltd., Hong Kong
This book was printed on totally chlorine-free Nymolla
Matte Art paper.
Production supervision by Ginger Boyer
Designed by Ivan Holmes

For Bob

—J. S.

For Liz Van Doren, who gave me the key to
a wonderful zoo

—B. S.

We asked Miss Darling, "May we get
A truly awesome classroom pet?"
She answered, "Yes! Or better yet,
Let's choose a whole pet alphabet."

Amanda Anaconda

Amanda Anaconda is our pet for letter A.
We think Amanda's wonderful in every
    single way.
She's nicer than an aardvark or an ant
    or armadillo,
And at story time, each one of us can use
    her for a pillow.

Boring Beetle Bill

Our boring beetle's name is Bill.
Bill's jaws are sharp for drilling.
He tunneled through Miss Darling's chair.
He found the flavor thrilling.
The chair collapsed. Miss Darling fell.
She telephoned the carpenter.
Bill Beetle has a boring job now:
He's our pencil sharpener.

Claude the Cat

Presenting Claude, our classroom cat,
The famous feline acrobat.
At 9:15 Claude takes a walk
Across the chalkboard to the clock,
Salutes the flag, then grabs the pole,
Performs a triple forward roll,
Lands neatly on Miss Darling's lap,
Curls up, and purrs, and takes a nap.

Our Dog, Doug

Do you think this is a rug?
Nope. It's really our dog, Doug.
He lets us roll him like a log.
(Doug's a very lazy dog.)
For exercise, he snores and slobbers.
Doug would never frighten robbers—
He couldn't even catch a slug.
What our dog, Doug, does best is hug.

Electric Eel

Please don't ask to feel
Our electric eel,
Because, if you bug him,
We cannot unplug him.

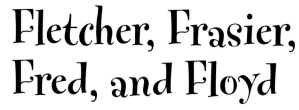

Fletcher, Frasier, Fred, and Floyd

They fly through the air
With the greatest of ease,
Using Claude the cat's tail
As a circus trapeze.
They're fabulous artists,
Yet Claude is not pleased.
No, it isn't much fun having fleas.

Gentle Jill

We have a guinea pig named Jill.
Jill's very good at standing still.
Why, sometimes she won't move for hours.
Who'd guess that she has superpowers?
Whenever we feel hurt or scared,
Whenever life is just unfair,
We find our guinea pig and pet her—
Bam! Shazam! We're feeling better.

Heaps of Hamsters

Have you seen our baby hamsters?
Why do hamsters always hide?
There is not a nook or cranny
That they cannot get inside.
I've found hamsters in my backpack,
In my sleeve and on my shoe,
In my pocket, in my mitten,
In my cup of carrot stew!
Oh! I think I know the reason
Why our hamsters want to roam:
They are bored with being at school,
And they want *us* to take them home.

Iggy Iguana

Meg put Iggy on her shoulder—
He's a super shoulder holder.
Moments later, he grew bolder,
And he climbed up on her head.

Now begins the part that's creepy—
Our iguana, feeling sleepy,
Made Meg's hair into a tepee,
And her head is now his bed!

Return to Sender: Jaguarundi

"Special delivery! Jaguarundi!"
The UPS man told us Monday.
He set the package on a shelf.
It growled!
      It roared!
           It opened itself!
A gentle pet this cat was *not*,
With jaws that bit and claws that caught.
We sadly sent her back and said,
"Let's get a jellyfish instead."

Katy Katydid

Our katydid kicked off the lid
Of her small cage, and then she hid.
We hear her singing,
>   *"Katydid,*
>   *Did-katy-katy-katy-did."*

Katy chirps the whole day long.
We're awfully tired of her song.
She won't stop singing,
>   *"Katydid,*
>   *Did-katy-katy-katy-did."*

Now when Miss Darling says, "Confess!
Who broke that rule? Who made this mess?"
Then every kid sings,
>   *"<u>Katy</u> did!*
>   *Did-katy-katy-<u>Katy</u> did!"*

Lunch-box Lemur

There's a lemur in my lunch box.
My banana's just a peel,
And my candy bar's a wrapper.
This is not a happy meal.

There's a lemur in my lunch box,
And I do not want her there!
Hmmm . . . She left me half a sandwich. . . .
It was nice of her to share.

Moosetake

We asked the pet shop for a mouse,
But by mistake they sent a moose.
A moose would mash our mouse's house,
And so we let him wander loose.

We're pleased to have a classroom moose,
Even though he's mighty large.
He holds our hats and coats and boots,
And usually, he doesn't charge.

Nick the Newt

Mister Smoot, our substitute,
Brought us Nick, the surfing newt.
Most newts just nap, but not our Nick.
Nick rides the waves on a Popsicle stick!

Otto Octopus

Otto is an octopus from underneath the sea,
And in our class he's learned a lot
    about geometry.
He couldn't wait to imitate a rectangle and
    pentagon.
He grew so bold he tried to fold into a
    hexaflexagon.
His tentacles got tied in knots. He could not
    move a muscle.
We spent two hours untangling our
    Otto octopuzzle.

Old Polly Parrot

Old Polly Parrot's the smartest of birds:
She knows more than 270 words
That she learned as the pet of a pirate
    named Kemper,
A man who, it's said, had a very bad temper.
Her first day in class, Polly opened her beak,
And was sent to the office for nearly a week.
Since then, because Polly's a sensible creature,
She only repeats words she hears from
    our teacher.

Quiet Quahog

We do not know our quahog well—
He always stays inside his shell.
Each time we knock, the door goes *slam!*
He's such an antisocial clam.

Our Rat Ralph

Our Ralph's a laboratory rat—
No rodent could be wiser—
And that's why we appointed him
Our science-fair adviser.

Ralph savors each experiment;
To please him is not easy.
And if you wish to win first prize,
Your project must be cheesy.

Scarlet Snake

Scarlet Snake is feeling scummy,
And she has a tummy ache.
Meanwhile we've been wondering
What happened to Kim's birthday cake.

Turkey Tom

Tom tumbled off the turkey truck;
We heard his frightened cries.
With Thanksgiving Day a week away,
Tom needed a disguise.

We dressed him in a suit and tie.
We thought he looked invincible.
Tom wandered down the hall and now
He's our assistant principal.

Umbrella Bird

Don't say a word.
Don't say a word.
Don't startle our umbrella bird!
This bird's so wide,
This bird's so flat,
Miss Darling wears him as a hat.
Please don't give
This bird a scare—
He might fly off and pull her hair.

SCHOOL

Vincent Vulture

On our field trip in December,
In the desert, far from culture,
Where most people never venture,
We went searching for a vulture.

Vincent circled high above us,
Seeking carcasses to crunch.
Could he ever learn to love us?
Yes, Miss Darling had a hunch.
She caught Vincent in an instant
With a three-week-old school lunch.

Will Warthog

Will warthog is not handsome,
His aroma is not sweet.
His hair is rough, his voice is gruff,
It's known he is not neat.
His tusks are rather hazardous,
His brain's not very big.
But what a boar! How we adore
This less-than-perfect pig!

Xenia the X-ray Fish

Xenia the x-ray fish
Swims serenely in a dish.
We like to sit and watch her dinner
When it is already in her.

Yorick the Yak

Yikes!
Yorick the yak is on the attack.
He's covering us with kisses.

Yuck!
The kiss of a yak is a huge gooey smack,
So we're very relieved when he misses.

Z???

We entered a contest to win a zorilla.
We thought it would be a kind of gorilla—
A warmhearted ape with plenty of spunk.
Surprise! A zorilla is only a skunk.

And since we got him, just why is it
No one ever comes to visit?

Ple-e-ease let us know if you should see
A better pet that starts with Z.